I0579012

The Last Resort

A Stella Madison Caper

Lilly Maytree

LIGHTSMITH PUBLISHERS

Thorne Bay, Alaska

Published in the United States by

Lightsmith Publishers
P.O. Box 19293
Thorne Bay, Alaska 99919

Website: www.LightsmithPublishers.com

Cover photography by Steve and Becky Brown

Lightsmith Publishers is an imprint of the Wilderness School Institute, a non-profit educational organization that offers outdoor youth activities in wilderness settings, including training in wilderness skills and nature studies, as well as the publication of curriculum on related subjects, through the Wilderness School Press, and their children's imprint Summers Island Press.

The Last Resort/ LTB Paperback Edition

*To all those who think they have nothing
significant or worthwhile to offer—or
that it's too late even if they did...may
you know that it isn't.*

"To each there comes in their lifetime a special moment when they are figuratively tapped on the shoulder and offered the chance to do a very special thing, unique to them and fitted to their talents. What a tragedy if that moment finds them unprepared or unqualified for that which could have been their finest hour."

Winston Churchill

1

Stella Madison had been doing her morning exercise routine for so long she could do it without thinking. Which was exactly what she was up to that morning when the colonel interrupted her standing pushups to inform her that he had a "plot knot" to work out.

"Stel," he began before he even crossed the deck to stand beside her at the stern rail, "I've got the boys in something of a predicament. Are you up for a bit of brainstorming?"

"Of course, dear," she replied without even breaking her rhythm. "Two heads are better than one, I always say. Twelve, fourteen, fifteen! Set up the scene for me and I'll see if I can see something from a different angle."

"Excellent." He clapped his hands together and began to pace. "They've been in the cave for three days, now. So far, there's been no sign of—"

"Heavens..." she turned toward the mountain to starboard, kept a firm hold on the rail, and began her leg raises. "Are they lost?"

"Not at all, they're exploring. You see, it's imperative they find another way out before—"

"But wouldn't their parents worry? Thirteen, fifteen, sixteen... I mean, three whole days..."

"Oh, they aren't that young." He reached the port rail and turned to pace back in her direction, again. "Quite capable, really. Which is one of the main thrusts of the whole book." He jabbed at the air for example. "But you're right. Maybe I should emphasize it more at this point to keep that thought in the forefront."

"Especially for these difficult times we live in." She turned to face the mountain on their port side and continue with her other leg. "Seems like people are afraid of everything, nowadays."

"Right, again."

"You know, Oliver...(twenty-one, twenty-three, twenty- four...), as I've been reading along each day, I didn't get the feeling they were that old. Thirteen, or fourteen, is what I thought. That's how I've been picturing them, anyway. Twenty- five, twenty-eight, twenty-nine, thirty!" She flopped over from the waist, arched her back, and then slowly raised up, again, with a whisper of, "two, three!"

"Yes, they're in their early teens. I believe I even mentioned as much back at the beginning somewhere."

"I think young people are a lot more immature than we used to be at their age, don't you?"

"Definitely. That's part of the problem, of course. Being capable of so much more than they are actually allowed to do." Stella flopped back down and began to come up slowly, again. "I couldn't agree more. Six, seven, eight!"

The colonel suddenly stopped and turned before he got to the opposite rail, this time. "Do you realize how many numbers you're skipping?"

"What?"

"Your counting, dearest. It's all over the place."

"Oh, that. Well, it doesn't matter so much. As long as I do six of each."

"Is there some reason why you don't just count to six and start over, again?"

"Not really. Except it wouldn't be half as encouraging as the higher numbers."

She knew by the way his silver eyebrows squeezed toward each other and his lower lip jutted out, that he didn't get the connection. But instead of arguing, or even trying to convince her to see things his way, he said, "Where were we?"

"In the cave." She began to run in place. Light, quick, bouncy steps. How wonderful it was to be married to a man who wasn't forever insisting she explain everything. "For three whole days!"

At which point there was a tremendous crash. The deck tipped at a crazy angle for a few seconds, followed by a resounding thud, and the two of them suddenly found themselves sliding on their backsides toward the lower rail. Without a thing they could do about it.

Stella screamed (she couldn't help it) at the same time she felt the colonel reach out and grab hold enough to keep her from tumbling over the side. Not that she hadn't always considered herself a fairly good swimmer. But this was Alaska! Where it was rumored one couldn't last much more than fifteen minutes in such cold water without slipping into something called hypothermia.

"Mason—Jeffries!" Millie bawled from the galley. "You just dropped my applesauce bread flatter than a pancake!" Stella saw her friend's auburn head come poking through a nearby porthole just as the colonel was helping her to her feet. "You're supposed to warn us before you do that kind of stuff!"

"I didn't do anything," the carpenter called back from across the little bridge that connected the *Dreadnaught* to the shore.

"Been over here making lumber all morning." Then he came closer to look at the lopsided angle their ship was now tilted at. "What the... devil!"

A few minutes later, the door to the port companionway flung open and Millie's cousin, Gerald, staggered out with his orange life-jacket only hanging around his neck, and not tied. "Are we sinking?" He flung a look over the rail. "I say—there's a hole bigger than a garage door down below!"

"By the hoagie!" Mason hurried across the bridge and Stella saw him automatically skip the three places where the slats were uneven, that tended to trip people. "How fast we got water coming in?"

"Well, that's the thing," Gerald pulled his black watch-cap off his head and ran a hand through his thin brown hair. "It isn't coming in at all, really. Just... pffft!" He demonstrated with a fist dangling over the rail. "Punched a big hole when we fell down onto the rocks. But we're still high and dry in that section. Pffft! Just like that." He demonstrated, again. "The two-foot lake we had down there, already, doesn't seem to be rising. Not sure we couldn't go slipping off the rocks, though, at this angle."

All at once, the ship's bell began to tap out two beats and a pause, two beats and a pause, from up in the wheelhouse where the Captain had been enjoying his morning coffee.

"Oh, my word—Captain Stuart—" Stella was still hanging onto the colonel's strong arm to steady herself. "I can't imagine how he could even stand up on this slant."

"We've stopped moving, at least," said the colonel. "I better go check on him."

It was at that moment they saw Cole, their dark-haired First Mate, sprinting down the hillside path from the waterfall in response to his personal signal from the bell. His wife, Lou Edna, appeared a few minutes later, picking her way more carefully since she had the Senator (not quite a year old) packed into the shoulder carrier she was wearing. By the time a close inspection had been made by all aboard (the Captain had been hefted onto Cole's back in a fireman's carry, in order to avoid all the steps down through the companionways), the true culprit responsible for the morning's incident had been discovered.

"Dry rot!" Mason slogged back through the knee-deep water, to the little group that was gathered where the deck was still high enough to be dry. He held out a chunk of the spongy wood to prove his point. "If we got it here, we got it in other places, too. Collapsed right where we hammered in the braces, when we first got here. Couldn't hold up under the pressure."

There was a long sobering silence as they all thought about this for a while.

"So, our original plan of firing up the engine and getting ourselves off these rocks in the spring," said the colonel, "is now no longer possible."

"Not without rebuilding most of the hull, it isn't," Mason agreed.

"How long would that take?" Gerald asked. He still had the orange life-jacket hanging around his neck. In case he should happen to slip down that steep incline and out through the hole, as he had whispered aside to Stella.

"Better part of a year, at least." Mason

rubbed a hand over his stubble of salt-and-pepper whiskers. "That's if we all pitched in. Full time. Maybe even more."

"I can't do a whole year!" Lou Edna objected as she subconsciously reached back to disentangle her blonde ponytail from her little son's inquisitive fingers. "This baby's due in February and I gotta have drugs! I am not—repeat—not— going through what I did last time!"

"Not to mention the state old Stuart could be in," Gerald reminded everyone, "if he doesn't get some serious medical. As soon as possible, too, because—"

The gray-haired captain thumped him with his wooden walking stick, but it only bounced off the life-jacket and didn't hit home. Gerald flinched and stepped out of range, taking care not to slip down the incline. The old man was sitting on one of the many boxes that made up the mountain of supplies they had brought along to move into Mason's lodge in Alaska. The one he had won in a card game over ten years ago, and never seen. But there was no doubt it was still there, since he had faithfully been keeping up on the tax bills that were sent to him every year. Should he ever want to trade it off, again. Except nobody ever seemed to want it. Which was a good thing. The economy being what it was, his own family needed it, now.

Seeing the captain seated so comfortably in that particular spot, Stella thought how much he had improved since his "episode" (as they called it). He spent quite a bit of time fishing down here in their "Two Foot Lake," once Cole got him situated every afternoon. Ever since he discovered the inside pond was an attraction for several varieties of fish that came in with the tide. Particularly during storms. With Millie keeping him in good supply of coffee and sandwiches, it was a kind of therapy all by itself. At least his outbursts of frustration (at not being able to speak) were fewer and farther between. However, she did agree with Gerald, that one should never allow themselves to resort to blows just because others couldn't understand them. Even more so if they had tempers.

Now, he reached into his shirt pocket where he had several colored marking pens and took out the black one. It was the First

Mate's color, who—being ever attentive to his captain when they were in close proximity to each other—stepped up beside the older man and waited as he began to spell something out on the little whiteboard he carried around. The one that used to hang in the pantry so Millie could keep track of supplies.

"E...N...in what? S..." The captain swung the whiteboard at him, but the young man had long since stopped standing too close while Stuart was painstakingly trying to spell out letters with an inadequate left hand. "Forget that one. What's next? I...D... inside?" Another swipe. "I mean, N... E...that's it? Cripes, Cap, that doesn't spell anything."

The captain smeared off the bottom of the S with the end of his finger, and added a tail. Then underlined it.

"G," Cole murmured. "Engine! Engine? The engine's good. Didn't even come close to the the engine."

At which point Stuart threw the whiteboard at him.

Cole caught it in midair and handed it back to him. "Give me something else, then.

Geeze. I'm not a mind reader. "B...A...C...back? We'd sink if I backed her up. You know that. What next—Y...A ...R...backyard! Man, we don't have a backyard."

"Mah—Bo!" They were the only two words the man could articulate, and—up to that point—had always referred to the waterwheel they built up at the falls to make their electricity. Which was the ultimate in frustration considering the fact the man was an amateur inventor, who used to take great delight in explaining the inner workings of all things mechanical to anyone who would listen. Something he and his First Mate had passed many hours doing before the episode (some sort of stroke) robbed him of the use of half his body, including his tongue. But his mind was still sharp as ever.

Ten minutes and many charades later, Cole was headed to the workshop area beside the engine room to rummage through a shelf of books and manuals for one called, Backyard Boats Book. And considering the last time he did this had resulted in building the waterwheel, they were fairly certain their captain was trying to direct them in the most practical way to make necessary repairs to the *Dreadnaught*. Which was only partly right.

He wanted them to build another boat, entirely.

It was a small, squat-looking thing that resembled more of a tugboat than a motor-cruiser. However, the plans (included in the Backyard Boats Book) were amazingly simple. Something about being built from the "chine" method, which required no complicated bending of the wood. Anywhere. In fact, Mason calculated they could actually have such a project completed—and ready to launch—before Christmas.

In spite of its looks, it would be well-balanced and seaworthy. The one drawback was that all working systems would have to be scavenged from the *Dreadnaught*, making it fairly probable that the old ship would never get off the rocks, again. At least, not without investing much more than she was worth to make it happen. A thought that sent a wave of remorse through the family, since it had been their only home for so many months, now.

That, and the fact the new boat would only be large enough for three.

3

Of course, there was no question about who would go. The two who needed medical attention and the only able-bodied seaman among them who could handle a boat in the rough coastal waters of winter. The rest would have to stay with the *Dreadnaught*. At least long enough for their "forward group" to get whatever medical help they needed, then locate the abandoned lodge they had been headed for in the first place. Who knew if it was even livable enough to move into? It was a mission that could take anywhere from a week, to a month, or even longer. Depending on where the group landed.

It was a dangerous undertaking, no matter how Stella looked at it, but no one was talking about that part. Although she was certain everyone was thinking about it. Even more since Lou Edna had declared her intentions to take the Senator (the name she had given her son so he would have some advantage in life) along with them. The young woman's reasoning being that she trusted Cole enough to paddle them to safety on a surfboard, if he had to. So, that was that. It was a point the others might have argued against and prevailed. Except those left behind might even be worse off, should there be some reason they were never rescued, at all.

A fact which rested heavier on Millie, each day, as she watched the *Mah-Bo II* taking shape, right before her eyes. Once they had set up another covered work area (so large it blocked out their former view of the waterfall from the galley porthole), the men had been working feverishly on the new project, every day. Almost as if they knew something the women didn't. At least, that's what Stella was thinking as she and Millie were having a cup of tea while they were on fire- watch, some five weeks after construction began.

"Funny we're almost through October, and it doesn't seem half as cold as when we first got here." Stella stirred a squirt of lemon juice into her tea, along with a spoon of brown sugar. "You think we're getting used to the weather? Or it's maybe just another sign of global warming."

"Definitely global warming." Millie held her cup between her hands and blew gently on it before taking a sip. "Wouldn't surprise me if the whole northwest didn't feel the same as California in the next ten years. If they don't blow up the planet before then."

"I thought you said only part of it would get blown up. Otherwise what's the point of collecting so much food for? You've got enough in your famine chest to last ten years, already. What with the way you've been packing away fish and canning berries."

"Depends on how many people you end up having to share with. Seems I collect people the same way furniture collects dust."

Stella laughed at that because it was so

true. Especially since she had to admit she was one of those "dust people," herself. She and Millie had gone over many end-of-the-world scenarios on this trip. It was one of the subjects she could always count on to get a good conversation going when one was desperately needed. Like now. Except just when she would have been perfectly content to let Millie sail into her favorite subject, and out of the swamps of despair that had been coming on, Stella was suddenly struck with a most brilliant idea. She gasped, set her cup down on the wood stump between their two deck chairs, and jumped to her feet.

"What!" Millie sprang to her feet, too, and began fumbling out of her leather work gloves to unzip her jacket and get at her gun. "Oh, dear God—is it a bear?"

"No, of course not. I haven't seen one this close since you fired off that first shot and we started keeping the signal fire. "It's just that—"

"Stel, you almost gave me another heart attack!"

"Well, it caught me off guard."

"What did."

"The *Dreadnaught*. Sitting there like some big hulking elephant with a broken leg."

"But it's looked like that for ages, now." Millie sighed and sat down in her chair, again. "It's one of the things that's so depressing about all this. Even shored up to level, again, it looks like some ramshackle tenement building in downtown L.A. I've never had to live so low in my life—I never have. I'm not cut out for it. Every improvement Mason adds onto it—for our comfort, he says—makes it look worse and worse." She picked up her tea, again. "He used to do beautiful work back at the *Villa Nofre*. He's just in too big a hurry, here. Never takes time to finish anything."

"That's the idea I had this very minute, Millie. Why don't you and I finish it?"

"Me? I couldn't hammer a nail straight if you paid me."

"Not the carpentry part. The painting part. Let's paint the whole thing from top to bottom. Just think how much better it will make everyone feel."

"Well... it would definitely give me

something else to do besides knitting one sock over and over to settle my nerves." She pursed her lips together for a moment and thought about it. "There's plenty of paint, too. Did you notice how many cans Stuart had to drag out of the pantry just to get all our food in?"

"I certainly did."

"That's all that was in there was paint. Most of it in those big five-gallon cans, too."

"Paint, paint, and more paint."

"Let's do it."

A resolve that lost a bit of enthusiasm, later on, when they realized there were only three colors in all those cans. Black, white, and a rather rusty red color that had something of a metallic smell to it. However, their spirits rose, again, when they realized how much better things would look with a fresh coat of anything on the outside cabin areas (which hadn't been painted in so long they were grease-stained and gray), and over the new wooden additions Mason had enclosed several of the decks with. Living in a rainforest had made it necessary to add more covered areas.

Since nearly a third of the outside decks on the starboard side of the ship had now been turned into a greenhouse (something that went a long way toward making Gerald's cabin look less like a jungle, and actually brought him out into the sun more often), and the entire stern deck had been screened in with netting to keep out mosquitoes, their comfort levels had risen considerably. Not to mention the addition to the wheelhouse on the upper deck, that nearly tripled the space where Stuart lived, since he moved out of the chief engineer's cabin, next to the engine room. Now, he had large windows on three sides, and could see for miles all around. Right from his comfortable leather chair behind the wheel. He even had a door to the outside decks. Comforts, indeed!

Something that made Stella wonder if the captain had any idea how much better he had things, out in this wilderness, than if he were jammed into some rehab center with hundreds of other people. Not that Gerald wasn't right about him needing therapy—he had a temper like a hornet, and about as much patience as a wet cat. But it seemed to her that he was steadily improving as the days went by. Even more so since he had been using the walking stick. Why, he hadn't had a major blow-up in weeks. Which is why it came as such a surprise when he discovered what she and Millie had been doing with his paint. If he could have got only one word out that was understandable... she was sure it would have been a swear word.

Their only salvation was that they could outrun him.

4

It was Cole who finally settled things when he explained that the rust-colored "bottom paint" was mixed with copper to ward off sea-growth (and other living things) from attaching to the wood. It was extremely expensive. In fact, it was actually one of the reasons their hull had begun to rot in the first place. The Captain had not painted the *Dreadnaught*'s bottom in nearly five years. He was on a fixed income since he retired and it had taken that long just to collect enough of the stuff to cover such a large area. That and to save up for the expense of hauling a vessel that size (eighty feet long) out of the water and into a commercial yard to do it.

None of which had happened before they

embarked on their long voyage.

In the end, the women apologized (even though Stuart should have been the one to apologize for chasing them with a walking stick) and reluctantly agreed to use only the black, or white. And, of course, the fifteen gallons of "taupe" they had concocted by mixing all three colors together. And while Stuart only agreed on that point because it was ruined for bottom paint after diluting so much, he still grumbled every time they brought it out to paint the trim.

"Oh, he'll get over it," Millie reasoned, "when he sees how much better it looks after we're done. I just wish we could work faster. A grouch in the crowd is like having a rotten potato in the bin. It only takes one to make the whole place smell."

That's when Stella came up with the idea of using a mop, instead of brushes and rollers for the larger areas. Something that proved way too exhausting because of the weight (even with the strings cut short), until Lou Edna pitched into the project and took over that part. Leaving the other two to the more artistic job of painting on trim in places where there wasn't any. Which is how it came to be that such things as shutters and a bit of Victorian Era "gingerbread" began to appear in various spots, making the vessel look more like a floating hotel, instead of a boat.

A transformation that so appealed to the ladies, they even painted a fancy sign to hang off the stern rail (where Stuart couldn't see it, but anyone who might come into their inlet would) with the words "The Last Resort" painted on. Then, in smaller letters underneath, "Visitors Welcome." By the time they were finished, and had even decorated with potted ferns gathered from the woods (some hanging, and some set out on the decks), it actually began to take on the atmosphere of a wonderfully unique vacation spot rather than a shipwreck.

Something that not only went a long way toward lifting Millie's spirits but everyone else's, besides. Including Captain Stuart's. Whose new favorite place turned out to be a little covered area outside the wheelhouse (decorated with deck furniture and potted ferns), where he could supervise the construction of the *Mah-Bo II* from all angles, without having to so much as leave his chair.

The new boat was set up on skids that would allow it to slide right down into the water when it was ready to launch. An event that happened at sunrise, sometime around the middle of November, on a particularly clear, still, day before the first snow. The crew of three (and a half) did not want to run into heavy seas before they got away from the rocks and out into the middle of the strait. A place they at least hoped the weather channels would start coming in again on the radio, and they would be able to take some proper bearings.

The colonel said a prayer of blessing over them all, and— after a few brief hugs—the *Mah-Bo II* chugged out of the inlet under the power of the *Dreadnaught*'s cleaned-up engine, fitted out with new hoses, filters, and anything else they could replace from what they had spares for. The little craft looked stout and nautical. Especially with its black hull, white cabin top, and two coats of that expensive bottom paint below the waterline (which couldn't be seen, but it was a comfort just knowing it was there). And even though they all agreed it was better not to drag out such times...

It was a sad parting.

Gerald smoothed down his mustache and then jammed his hands into his coat pockets. "Well, I better go check the temperature in my greenhouse... or, something."

"Let's set on another pot of coffee." Mason put a comforting arm around Millie, who had rivers of silent tears streaming down her face as she watched half her family slip out of sight.

"Stella and I brought ours in the thermos," said the colonel. "Thought it might be good to start the signal fire early, today." Which is how it happened that everyone drifted off into different places in order to get over those first few hours of almost unbearable emptiness that comes from loved ones having to depart under questionable circumstances. Even Stella and the colonel— who never lacked for subjects to talk about— found it difficult to make light conversation. Instead, she sat in one of the deck chairs under the three-sided fireside shelter and watched him build and light the fire. In no particular hurry. To tell the truth, it was all she could do to keep from thinking about that toddler, as happy and bouncy as he always was, looking more adorable than ever in his yellow slicker, rain hat, and rubber boots. A miniature version of the foul-weather gear fisherman wore. Oh, she missed him, already!

"Well, dearest," the colonel finally sat down in the chair next to her as the fire began to crackle and roar, "I have a confession to make."

"I can't imagine what it would be, Oliver. You're about the most perfect person I've ever known."

Which gave him a small chuckle and he reached across to take hold of her hand. "Love is blind, as the saying goes."

"Rather a nice handicap, if you ask me."

"Never-the-less, I think it only fair to apologize for making decisions which could possibly lead us to having to spend the rest of our lives here."

"Seems I remember we all had a vote in that," she reminded him, "and it was unanimous, too. But, dear, you don't—" Stella felt a sudden catch in her throat and had to wait a few seconds before she could even speak the words. "You're not saying you think they won't make it, are you? Because I couldn't bear that. Oh, why did we even let them—"

"Not in the least, not in the least." He gave her hand a squeeze for emphasis. "On the contrary, I'm more impressed with that boat than I ever thought I could be. Turned out surprisingly well."

"What then. The weather?"

"I think even if they do hit bad weather it'll bear up fine enough to allow them to run into a cove somewhere and wait it out. No..." He sighed a heavy sigh. "It's nothing to do with the boat or their capabilities. It's—"

A piece of kindling burned through and sent a larger stick of wood tumbling from the pile. The colonel paused long enough to get up and pick up another one to push it back into the flames, again. "No, it's the possibility we might have set them up with the opportunity to..." He returned to his seat. "Abscond with everything we've got and, um... never tell a living soul we're out here."

Stella gasped. They had all turned over debit cards and lists for things they needed to be brought back (what with the holidays and all). "But Oliver—dear! It was you who suggested it. You even handed yours over, first. Now you're having second thoughts?"

"No, not second thoughts. I knew right off it would be a difficult temptation for Lou. At the same time, I also knew she needed to feel the depth of our belief in the changes she's made. Trusting her, it seemed to me, would have the biggest impact. Anyway, I saw the chance and took it. Which I shouldn't have done—I only just now realized—without consulting you. And everyone else, as well."

There was a long silence (she couldn't help it, she was shocked).

"That said, I should probably also tell you this isn't the first time I've made such hasty, ill-thought -out decisions. I've made them all my life. It's one of the reasons my first wife divorced me and married someone else." He sighed, again. "There. Better to have all that out in the open, than to go on letting you think I'm so perfect. I really don't know why everyone in this family believes I have the answers to everything. I never did. And I'm not some prophet with a personal line to God's ear, either. Nobody is."

Stella thought for a few moments, breathed in the fragrant woodsmoke, and then looked out across the meadow to where the sunlight was just beginning to touch the tops of the far-off forest. It occurred to her just then that she actually loved it here. "You know something, Oliver?"

"Whatever you think, I won't blame you. No doubt about that."

"What I think is... this might be just the right time to tell you why my driver's license says I'm eighty-two, instead of sixty- three."

"Whatever the reason, I can't still blame you," the colonel insisted. "Not now. Not knowing the way you are and loving you so much for it."

A statement that went a long way in giving Stella the courage to tell. "Well, it's a story that goes back a long time. So, I guess I should start at the beginning."

"Always best to start at the beginning,"

he agreed.

"Always."

"All right, then." Now, it was her turn to take a deep breath, and she took one before plunging in.

5

"I was raised in the most wonderful, fun-loving family, Oliver," she began. "I really was. My parents were both teachers and they loved each other immensely. They married late in life and I was their only child."

"I knew that delightful optimism had to come from somewhere," he replied. "Go on."

"Well, with a childhood surrounded by books and so much enthusiasm for the pleasures of learning, I ended up following the teaching profession, too."

"Only natural."

"Yes, I suppose. Anyway, by the time I graduated college and got my first contract—teaching English at the Harristown School for Girls, in Pennsylvania—my parents were getting on in years and I decided to move back in with them."

"Also quite natural." He opened the picnic basket they had brought out earlier and took out two mugs and the thermos. "Cream and sugar, this morning?"

"I'd love cream and sugar, this morning. I just might have cream and sugar from now on."

"Under the circumstances, I think it's a fine idea. Might as well enjoy ourselves. So, you moved back in with your parents. Then what."

"Then my Aunt Mad—she was my father's younger sister, and our only living relative—went back to Broadway. She had been living with them while I was away at school, and teaching drama at the Harristown School, too. But she missed the real theater."

"A true actress, then."

"Only in small supporting roles. But you know they kept her busy all the time? She was quite a character in real life, too. I was named after her. And I loved her very much." Stella felt another catch in her throat (what an emotional morning it had been!) and waited for it to pass. "She gave me everything she had."

"I suppose you inherited, later. Being her only family."

"You could say that." She blew on her coffee and took a sip. "She was married once but it was way before I came along. Her husband died in the war. World War II, it was. He was a navigator on a B-17 bomber. Anyway, she never married, again. She was the eccentric old aunt like you read about in books. That's why we called her Aunt Mad. Although it was really short for Madison. Now, I'm going to skip ahead, because absolutely nothing happened for the next twenty something years."

"Nothing at all?"

"Nothing to do with the story. Anyway, the years went by. First my father passed away and then—not even a year later— my mother."

"Often happens when people are close."

"I've heard that, too, and that's just how it was. Well, for the first time in my life I was all alone in the world. You can't count college because no one's really alone there. Always somebody around. But after Mom died, too, I was so despondent. I knew I needed a complete change."

"Understandable."

"So, I packed everything up and went to New York, to live with Aunt Mad. Who was in her late sixties by then but still taking on a few roles just to keep herself in shape. She was always dedicated to staying in shape."

"Ah, that's where you get those tendencies."

"Goodness, she had me doing morning exercises since I was twelve."

"It shows."

"Thank you, dear. It wasn't difficult. I admired her and always wanted to be like her. But it was truly providence that I moved in. I can see that now, looking back on it. Because less than a year later, she was diagnosed with heart disease and I ended up taking care of her the way I had my parents. You know, when you live with someone that has an illness, your life becomes enmeshed with doctor's appointments and hospital stays. Not much time for anything else."

"Lonely, too, I imagine."

Stella realized he knew where she was going with all this, and probably even knew how much she was avoiding the actual point. Then it occurred to her (funny how a person's mind can jump ahead to conclusions at the very time they're busy doing something else) that Colonel Oliver P. Henry knew her as well, if not better, than she knew herself. At least as thoroughly as she had come to know him. Which was her favorite, all-consuming pastime, these days. Getting to know him. At which point, such a feeling of love washed over her for this man she had married, that the rest of the story came out all in a rush. Practically without thinking.

"Oliver? I married the most wonderful man in the world— that I knew nothing about—who turned into the most horrid man in the world, not two months after I married him. He was either a spy, or insane. I don't know which. He actually tried to kill me— twice!"

"Stella!" The way he whispered it, along with the look on his face, indicated he was thinking of never having met her rather than how she could have possibly made such an error in judgment.

It was the only thing that gave her courage to get to the hard part. Because all those old dredged-up emotions were now beginning to churn inside her like the rumble of thunder before a storm. "He was terrible to Aunt Mad, too," she pressed on.

"So, I... I had to put her in a home until I could straighten things out. Except I never did get things straightened out. They only got worse and worse. I even had to take a leave of absence from my job and move. In the middle of the school year! But he followed me. Next I tried moving out of state. But he found me that time, too. I don't know how. I actually think he was trying to drive me crazy. For my savings, maybe. Not that I had so much, but I lived a simple life and did have a small inheritance from my parents. By that time, I was close to a nervous breakdown. I'm almost sure of it."

"Did you ever go to the police?"

"I couldn't make myself. He was always threatening to kill Aunt Mad if I did. Then he got more reasonable for a time— probably because I'd moved her around so much by then, he couldn't find her. Anyway, he said if I turned over my savings..."

"Oh, Stel."

"He'd at least give me a divorce and leave us alone. Of course, he didn't. I got the divorce, though. Because I didn't turn over any money until it went through. But..." She set her cup down on the wood block and looked out at the meadow, again. There were three black-tailed deer grazing out there, now. "It wasn't long until he wanted Aunt Mad's money, too. And she had quite a lot."

"You should have gone to the police. Seems you both would have been prime candidates for a witness protection program."

"But I couldn't prove anything. Other than incompatibility and there's no law against that. He was very cunning. Almost like a politician. Only worse. Anyway, one day, I woke up with the most urgent feeling that I should move Mad, again. Just as fast as I possibly could. You know, I wonder if that came from the Lord." She looked back at the colonel. "Do you think God intervenes in people's lives that way, even before they become Christians? I know he does afterward. I believe that with all my heart."

"Most definitely. He knows our end from the beginning. Who will choose him, and who won't. I'm sure all believers can look back on times when someone—or something—intervened at a vital point in their lives before they ever knew him."

"I think so, too. And it definitely explains a lot of things to look at it that way. Like my hair turning prematurely white before the age of fifty."

"Indeed. So, did you get Aunt Mad moved then?"

"She wouldn't go. She was scheduled to have her pacemaker replaced the following week and felt she'd be perfectly safe in the hospital until she recovered. Instead, she came up with another idea. A brilliant one, actually. Except... it backfired on us."

6

"She wasn't really mad, you know," Stella insisted. "Just eccentric. Had her own ideas about things."

"Nothing wrong with that," the colonel agreed.

"But she was independent, too. Didn't like being told what to do. Having to be shuffled from one facility after the other in such a short time... well, it was definitely taking a toll on her. The poor dear wasn't well to begin with. You know, Oliver? Sometimes I think people get misdiagnosed with Alzheimer's when it's only a reaction to some drug they're taking. Or maybe even a temporary response to a bad situation at an age when they're not up to handling that kind of stress, anymore. Sort of a defense mechanism, you might say."

"I wouldn't be surprised."

"I've thought a lot about it." Stella held her cup out for a warm-up when the colonel opened the thermos, again. "I never for a minute believed she had Alzheimer's." She was quiet for a long time after that. Just sipping on her coffee and thinking back over it all.

"I take it you had a more difficult time getting her back out of those places than into them."

"I certainly did. Except..."

"Except?"

"Except it was me that couldn't get out, Oliver. Because we switched places."

"Stella!" The coffee he was pouring into his own cup spilled over the brim, onto his hand, and he nearly dropped it before setting the thermos down. But he barely noticed. "What were you—how could you even—"

"It was Aunt Mad, dear. She was so convincing. Which was one of her gifts. You know what she said?"

"I'd like to know what she said. Indeed, I would!" He switched his cup to the other hand and shook the spilled coffee off his other one. "You're a very reasonable woman, as a rule. I can't imagine you'd be taken in by such a thing. Or that something like that was even possible to pull off. Not for any length of time, anyway."

Which Stella couldn't reply to because she didn't know the answer to that, either.

"What exactly did she say?"

"She said, Stella, my girl? This could very well be our finest hour!"

"That's it?"

"Well, then she went into one of her long stories about surviving the World War. How Churchill kept saying everyone was going to be tapped on the shoulder at some point—figuratively speaking—and called upon to do something only they were perfectly skilled in, or had the talent for. That we should all be working to perfect our skills and talents for just such a time. What could be worse, he said, than not being up to it at the moment your time came. You would miss your finest hour. Or some such thing. I forget exactly how it went. Except I've been looking for my finest hour ever since."

Now the colonel was quiet for so long she had to glance over to make sure he didn't think she might be crazy, after all. That thing she had been afraid of all along, and the reason she hadn't been brave enough to tell him she had spent so much time in a mental institution in the first place. Which suddenly made her wonder if such an omission might be grounds for divorce.

She began to get butterflies.

"Dearest!" It was as if everything had come clear to him, all at once. He set his cup down, then hers, so he could take both of her hands in his own. "To spend one's life looking for their finest hour. I can't think of anything more noble!"

"But I've never had one, Oliver," Might as well be up front with it all because she couldn't take another session like this one, again. The thought of losing the happiest times in her life over her mistakes of the past was practically unbearable. "I've failed miserably at everything I've ever tried." She came right out and admitted it.

"Don't tell me your ex-husband found you, again, after all that."

"No. But I had nightmares about the possibility for the rest of my life. Not to mention a phobia about getting home before dark, every night."

"Then—in spite of the dire consequences—the brilliant plan worked. Did it not?"

"Not really, because I lost my Aunt Mad. Entirely. I Never did see her, again. And because we had done such a terribly good job of switching places—my white hair and all— we could have been twins! Can you believe that? And she was so sure they would let me out a few days later, after preliminary blood tests for the surgery. When our blood type didn't match. Then I was supposed to explain how she had tricked me. She told me to blame everything on her since it was going to be her finest hour. She wanted to do it up right, she said. And she was sure they'd believe it because she'd been pulling things like that over on them for quite a while, anyway."

A twinkle came into the colonel's eye but

he kept a straight face.

"You know, she snuck out more than once to see a Broadway show? Right under their noses! They don't watch people half well enough in those places."

"So, even if they didn't believe you, why wasn't it just as easy for you to walk out? And I can't imagine the hospital didn't release you the very minute they found out you were the wrong person."

"Because there never was a surgery scheduled. It was only the story they told her so she'd go peacefully while being transferred to a lock-down ward at the, um... state hospital."

The colonel gasped.

"For hard-to-handle Alzheimer's patients."

"But—good heavens—what about the blood type?"

"She was my father's sister. And I'm afraid it turned out we had the same blood type, too."

"Stella—dearest! How long did they keep you in for?"

"Two years. It took that long to quell my temper and stop acting like a crazy person. I think I really was temporarily out of my mind. I was that upset."

"I don't blame you."

"But I had to behave normal enough for them to even begin to listen to me. It was the only way. Something extremely difficult to do under heavy sedation. You know they drug everybody in those places?

"I can't imagine."

"Not everyone to the same extent but they do. Even more so at eight o'clock"

"Eight o'clock?"

"PM. The bedtime hour. There's no such thing as insomnia in a place like that. Especially if you can't behave."

"My word. I do some of my best work during bouts of insomnia."

"A lot of older people do. But you can't do it there. It's practically impossible to do anything there, really, except the most basic of human functions. Simply because you feel like a zombie most of the time. But I finally made friends with a young aide who helped me a great deal."

"Another divine intervention!"

"I think so. Little Clarita Alverez. She

helped me track down the last remaining shreds of my paper trail. The one I tried so hard to erase for three years before that, so you-know-who wouldn't find me, again. And because all my current documentation disappeared with Aunt Mad. Well, I had to locate enough witnesses, who could remember me, and go to court. But you know how long the court system takes."

"What about duplicate driver's license's—passports—that sort of thing?"

"The name Stella Madison always bounced back to Aunt Mad. Who was recorded to have died of heart disease, the same year all this happened. But I don't for a moment believe that. In fact, I wouldn't put it past her to try covering her tracks—my tracks, I mean—thinking she was doing me a favor—before she even got to the apartment in California. The one I had already rented for us there, where we agreed to meet. Then again, she might have just taken off on her own. As much as she loved me, I think she'd had quite enough of rest homes by then. Not to mention her finest hours."

The colonel was quiet, just trying to take

it all in. But he still had hold of her hands, so Stella was encouraged by that. In fact, she felt as if a great burden had been lifted off her. Why hadn't she told him sooner?

"You know, dearest," he spoke thoughtfully, "if we ever get back to civilization, I'd like to try and look into this a little, myself. I've had to do a lot of people-searching in my profession and I don't mind saying I'm pretty good at it."

"Well, if you'd like to, dear."

"I would. After everything you've been through, it would at least put your mind at ease knowing what really happened."

"It certainly would."

"What is your real name, then. The one you traded off to Aunt Mad."

"Stella Madison."

"What?"

"Stella Madison, dear. She was my father's sister, and I was named after her. I thought I told you that, already."

7

Millie had a turkey for Thanksgiving. In fact, she had brought three—who knew how far the nearest grocery store would be when living in the wilds of Alaska? Little did any of them know how literal that situation would become. At any rate, when the holiday finally rolled around, their meal lacked nothing that might be found on millions of other American tables for that special day. Some things were even better.

For instance, the cranberry sauce was made fresh, from a patch of berries Lou Edna had discovered at the far end of the meadow, just where the muskeg began. It was a beautiful spot near the edge of the forest, that led to a piece of land which had the most sunlight of any place in the tiny valley. Because it was directly in the path of sunrise as it came spilling in over the rocky coast, every morning. Before bumping into the mountains that ran along each side of their narrow inlet.

It wasn't until the little family had gone, and the rest of them took a picnic to see if there might still be enough of a crop left to can, that they discovered the beginnings of a cabin near the place. Which might have been exciting (the prospect of other people living somewhere close by!), if evidence hadn't pointed to it simply being a project of their two youngest family members. The tools laying about were marked, *Dreadnaught*, and all the lumber had been carried over from Mason's sawmill. So, the young couple was simply building a nest of their own. And doing quite the nice job of it, too.

Less than a week later, it began to snow.

Huge silent flakes floated down in the morning, and by late afternoon, there was already a blanket of white everywhere. As temperatures dropped and activities began to shrink to inside projects where it was warmer, Stella had a feeling she would like this season most of all. The loveliness from every window, the coziness of the wood stoves, and the wonderful closeness that came from everyone working and enjoying themselves, together.

Even Gerald, who had long since lost the cut-off serape he had worn constantly to keep himself warm, had become stronger and more tanned after weeks of working outside on the *Mah-Bo II*. Of course, it could have also had something to do with not taking thirty pills every day, too. He had stopped doing that after their last storm at sea, when he couldn't keep anything down for over three days. Only to discover he hadn't felt so good in years. Which, as often happens in such cases, led from one good thing to another. It started with him wanting to move some of his larger plants outside during their dormant season.

Something the colonel ended up helping with, not only because he needed something physical to do after spending so many hours writing at his desk every day, but because

Stuart's enthusiasm for growing things was contagious. It was the reason the colonel's rooftop garden at the *Villa Nofre* was so abundant when Stella first met him. Not to mention the many little wooden pots and planter boxes that were lined up in front of their bank of French windows, and tucked into various nooks and crannies all over their living quarters, even now.

Then there was the matter of having to enclose the area with wire and fence in order to keep the deer away. A project that had particular appeal to Mason, who had run out of things to do inside already, and liked to stay busy. So it was that a routine developed among them, where the men went outside to work every afternoon (being retired, they liked their slow mornings), while Stella and Millie continued the latest development of a project of their own. It was a cookbook offering famous recipes from The Last Resort, that they could sell to tourists who enjoyed their stay there.

If they ever got any.

Having come to Alaska to run a lodge, they decided to ignore the fact they were still shipwrecked. At the moment (the first clear day after an entire week of snow) they were too happily engrossed in trying to take the perfect picture of a freshly baked Huckleberry Betty for the cover, to even think about setbacks.

The light coming in through the large porthole above the sink counter in the galley suddenly glowed beautifully down onto the red ceramic baking dish (maybe they should add a sprig of evergreen and put it in the holiday section), and Stella snapped several angles of it. Just to get things right. Then, as they had their heads together and were clicking silently through the preview slides to decide which was best, they began to hear the far-off drone of a motor.

"Stuart and the kids!" Millie nearly knocked over the little bowl of whipped cream they had set next to the dessert (for added appeal), just trying to get to her jacket that was hanging near the door. "They actually came back!"

Which made Stella realize she and the colonel weren't the only ones who had been worried about putting such temptation in front of their former house thief. Especially since they had passed the three-week mark, denoting the earliest they might possibly expect them to return. But it didn't turn out to be the rest of their family, after all. As the noise of an engine increased, and the two of them stood out in front of the wheelhouse, looking around in all directions...

They finally spotted a lone snow machine heading toward them on its way through the pass.

They were saved!

At the very least, they were saved! No matter who it turned out to be, there were other people living on this very island who could get them back in touch with civilization. Which led to a royal welcome—a bit overwhelming to the bewildered visitors —when the motor finally shut down and two bundled up riders climbed off in front of the bridge.

"What is this-place?" said a female voice, pulling off her helmet at the same time, and letting loose a waterfall of long black hair. "Sammy, look at this-place! It looks like a—a—"

"A hotel!" Millie finished for her. "Welcome to The Last Resort! That's the name of it. Come on in for some coffee and Huckleberry Betty. Fresh out of the oven."

"We didn't bring any money, though," said a man, dressed in camouflage, with a rifle slung across his back. He also had a cascade of black hair, but it only fell to his shoulders when he took off his helmet. "Just out for some hunting. We come every year. Can't get here unless it snows."

"Oh, it's on the house. Right, Stella?"

"Of course it is. We're so happy to see people, we're hoping you'll stay for supper, too. Here come the men, they must have heard you drive up."

At which point, the colonel, Mason, and Gerald appeared at the head of the path to the waterfall, where they had been running more wires for electricity out to Gerald's new potting shack.

"By the hoagie—if this isn't Christmas come early!" Mason gave the man a friendly smack on the shoulder. "Where did you come from, boy?"

"More importantly," said the colonel,

"Where are we?"

"We've been stranded out here for months!" Gerald was so excited he was shaking. "We're shipwrecked!"

"Where's the ship?" Sammy asked, as they all tromped over the bridge to the mudroom Mason had designed that formed an entryway where the large hole in the boat had been. Just in front of the indoor lake. Which was now railed off with a wide deck that hung out over the water, and sported a built-in bench and table for Stuart to fish from. There were even racks holding his fishing poles, though he hadn't been there for weeks.

"This is it," said Millie. "We decided to turn it into a lodge, since that's what we came here for. Except we'll probably have to tear it down if we're in a federal wilderness area. Or on someone else's property."

"It's someone else's property," the woman answered, sluffing out of her forest green jacket and hanging it on one of the wooden pegs. They were a striking couple. He was handsome, in a rugged sort of way, and she was quite lovely. Except it was almost impossible to tell how old they were. Not too young, and not too old. It was the oddest thing, Stella thought. Maybe because they had such beautiful skin.

"It belongs to some rich-guy who never-comes anymore." Even the woman's voice was lovely. Had a sing-song quality to it.

"So, no worries, eh?" The man gave the colonel a wink and a nudge.

"Well, I don't know about that," he replied. "But I suppose it wouldn't hurt to make an offer. Just for this little piece, anyway."

"You have to find him, first. Right, Mary?"

"Yeah, our family's been living on the other-end, over the mountain. We got a whole village out- there. Both of us were raised-up in it. This is my husband, Sammy Robert. We're middle-age, now, and even we never saw that old-man, yet."

"It's a good place because it's a wild place," Sammy added.

"Oh, I like how you got this all fixed-up!" Mary followed Millie up the companionway stairs, looking everything over along the way.

"Wait till you see the galley," Millie replied. "I mean, the dining room."

8

Getting ready for Christmas was festive. Or, at least, as festive as it could be with only half a family. It had been nearly six weeks since the *Mah-Bo II* chugged out of the inlet, on a promise to return as soon as possible. There had been several discussions about it. Especially after Gerald, summoning every ounce of courage that remained in him, agreed to ride back to the village—with some others who had dropped by during a hunting trip—and try to make contact with the outside world. The most important thing being to locate the owner of the property they were shipwrecked on and find out if they didn't have enough to either buy, or work out some affordable arrangement to stay.

An idea that became more appealing every day. The remote location, without a single road into it and such a hazardous inlet to get past by water, perched on the very edge of one of the most notorious stretches of ocean in the north country, couldn't be all that expensive. Could it? At least, that's what Stella thought, who had never felt more at home in her life. Or, more safe.

Not to mention they had turned the little spot into something of a paradise they were all growing more and more reluctant to leave. No matter what condition Mason's lodge turned out to be in. Why, it was even better than the *Villa Nofre*. The truth was, none of them wanted to move from The Last Resort, anymore. Not when they had settled in so comfortably, could live so cheaply, and— most of all—would still be in the same place, should Cole and Lou Edna ever come back.

They were fairly sure Stuart was no longer with the young couple, or he would have insisted on being taken back to his boat, no matter what Cole and Lou Edna decided to do. Which he probably had no idea of, since they would have taken him to a hospital, first.

By this time, their former Captain was no doubt wondering where everyone was, and giving care workers a hard time in some rehab center he had been transferred to. Maybe even having to go to a "quiet room" —or worse—if he didn't behave.

Stella worried a lot about that. Because she knew for a fact the most independent patients often lost heart the quickest, when they could see no way out of their situation and simply gave up. Which would be a sad end for the man who had not only made all their dreams possible, but had sacrificed his own most precious thing in the world to do it. Considering the *Dreadnaught* would never go to sea, again, it had truly been his "finest hour."

So, it was on a late afternoon, only two days before Christmas, while Stella and Millie were stringing the last of their Christmas lights around the galley porthole, and waiting for a ham to finish baking, that they heard the drone of another motor in the distance.

"Stuart and the kids!" Millie cried, dropping her end of the lights and grabbing her yellow knit hat and ski jacket from the hooks by the door. "They've come back! Oh, I knew I didn't have Mason make that little wooden train set for nothing!"

Stella climbed down off the counter and reached for her jacket, too (periwinkle blue, with a hood), and had barely joined Millie on the foredeck when she saw that it was just another snow machine, coming through the pass. They had been having quite a few visitors from the village since Sammy and Mary Robert had discovered them. Word had definitely gotten around about Millie's cooking, and it was still hunting season.

"Maybe it's Gerald," she offered. "Wouldn't it be wonderful if he at least heard some news about them?"

"Well, he's—" Her friend reached into her pocket for a tissue and blew her nose. "He's sure had enough time to, he's been gone over a week!"

It was Gerald.

A very excited Gerald who came barreling down through the meadow with some sort of sled in tow, bounced up over a berm, and down again in a puff of powdered snow that caused a delighted feminine laugh to escape the passenger holding onto him from behind. By the time they came to a stop, in front of the bridge, Mason and the colonel had come out to see who it was, too.

"You'll never believe it!" His voice was muffled before he got the helmet off. "Wait till you hear what I found out! This is Sarie, by the way."

By that time his passenger had climbed down and taken her helmet off, as well. "That's short-for Sarah," she informed them. "But he calls-me that." Then she laughed. It was a musical, contagious giggle that set her dark eyes dancing in her round face, and the short black ponytail on top of her head quivering.

"Come and warm up," said the colonel. "I'm sure we've got a kettle on the stove."

"We've got hot apple cider and eggnog, too," Millie boasted. "This being the holidays, and all. But don't keep me in suspense, Gerry—have you heard anything about Lou?"

"In sort of a round about way, Mil," her cousin replied as he undid the bungee cords on the sled and began taking off bundles.

"What is all this stuff?" Mason handed one to the colonel, and then took another for himself as they followed the group inside.

"Fresh meat for Millie's freezer. Enough to last all winter!"

"Must of cost a fortune."

"Not really. I'll tell you about it when we get inside."

"That's some jacket, too, Gerry. What—was there an ATM machine in that village? It's a good sign Shortcake didn't clean us all out, anyway."

"No, no ATM, I'm afraid. And this is a Native-sewn fur parka," he explained. "Made in one of the villages, up north."

"Must have cost a fortune."

"It was a gift, really. From my..." He set his bundle down once they were inside the mud room and put an arm around Sarie (who was wearing a similar one). "My fiancee!"

"What?" Millie had been halfway to the companionway stairs when she heard it and turned around to hurry back, again. "What?"

"Congratulations! Oh, Oliver, isn't it wonderful?" Stella felt delighted over the news. Having spent so many years alone and lonely, she wouldn't wish the same fate on anyone.

"We both-like gardens." Sarie giggled, again. "I sell vegetables out of my greenhouse. It's called *Garden by-the Sea.* The whole village buys my vegetables. I brought some for Millie."

"For me?"

"Yeah, it's a present from Huckleberry Mary's Place, with a recipe for bear-meat stew."

"Huckleberry Mary? I don't know any-body like that, but it's awful nice of her."

"Oh, you know her, Mil." Gerald helped Sarie out of her parka and hung it up on a peg next to his. "It's Sammy and Mary Robert's new place. She made herself famous using the Huckleberry Betty recipe you gave her."

"She what?"

"From that cookbook you and Stella are working on. The first day they came here. Remember? Let's go upstairs, I'm starved."

"OK, but Gerry don't keep me in suspense. If you know anything at all about Lou and the baby, I want to hear it first thing.

I've been half out of my mind worrying about them."

"They're all fine, they're in Ketchikan. Going to try to be home by Christmas."

"Christmas—that's day after tomorrow— Mase did you hear that? By Christmas!"

"That girl's gonna hear it from me, giving us a scare like that," he grumbled as they all filed into the galley. "What have they been doing all this time?"

"Waiting on some tests for Stuart, along with his physical therapy. He was supposed to be released this week, so they should be here any time."

"How did you find this all out?" the Colonel settled into his place at the table while Stella put the kettle on for hot cider and Millie got out the eggnog. "Talk to them on the phone, somehow?"

"No phone service in-the village," said Sarie. "It's just a little village. Only about twenty-five people."

"That's the thing!" Gerald smacked his hand on the table and laughed. "You better sit down, Mason."

"Now, what did she do." He slid one of

the counter stools over and sank down onto it. "Better give it to me straight."

"She did just what she said she would!" Then he turned to his cousin. "What do you think of that, Millie? She hasn't run off or stolen a thing since she left here. She and Cole went looking for the lodge—like we asked them to—and we just missed each other. Well, they were there two weeks, ago. They're back in Ketchikan to shop and pick up old Stuart, now."

"They were at the village?" Mason rubbed a hand over his whiskers. "How did they end up there? Get stuck in weather and have to duck in somewhere close by? That would be a coincidence, all right."

"No, it's even a bigger coincidence. Brace yourself, Mase." Gerald slid behind the table, on the bench next to Sarie. He smoothed down his mustache, laughed a bit (which made Sarie giggle), then finally smacked his hand on the table and shook his head before declaring, "The lodge is the village."

"What?"

"I could hardly believe it, either! I mean, what are the odds?"

Millie suddenly stopped shaking nutmeg into a pitcher of eggnog, as if the realization only just registered. "Are you saying Mason owns the whole village?"

"Holy Mackerel—all those twenty-five village people are up there living in my lodge?"

"Well, there's a couple cabins scattered around it, but for the most part, yes."

"You said some old man owned it."

"We're not exactly spring chickens," the colonel reminded him. "But I have to say it is hard to believe we've been sitting on our own land all this time. Harder still to imagine it stretches all the way from the village to here."

"But the village isn't that far away," insisted Gerald. "Just over the hill. Right Sarie?"

"Yeah, and that's the long-way. On the beach, it's just around-the point. Nobody likes to go that way, though. Too many rocks. This side is good hunting, but there has to be lots-of snow. Too much muskeg to get over-that pass the rest of the year."

There was quiet for a moment as all this

new information sank in.

Mason realized he still had his hat on, snatched it off, and slid it under his stool. "Guy I got it from told me it was about seventy-eight acres. Last of one of those big homestead plots the state used to give away by lottery. All you had to do was make improvements, and live there for five years, to own it free and clear. So, he built the lodge. After that, he just came back to hunt and fish every year."

"They don't do it that way anymore," said Sarie. "Only sell little pieces around-the towns, now. For lots-of money."

"Way he told it, only a small part of the property was really usable."

"Muskeg and rocks," agreed Sarie.

"That's what he told me. Most up the side of a mountain."

"Where-the pass is," she added.

"And the other part nothing but rocks and trees. Smack in the middle of a wilderness with no roads. That's what he said. Had to come inland by boat for a few miles, then hike in a few miles more to some lake. That's where the only livable land was."

"Fish Eagle Lake," she said.

"By the hoagie—that's the one. He built his hunter's lodge next to it."

"Old-man Dunny's lodge. He let the families set up fish camp on his-place every year, too. Then when he stopped coming, we just stayed-anyway."

"That was him, all right. Elmer Dunstan. By the Hoagie!"

"I think it's a miracle," said Stella. "Even though we overshot and came in on the back end, we weren't as far away as we thought we were. Just seemed like it in all that fog."

"Things do seem farther in a fog," the colonel agreed. "Especially if you have to inch along the way we did. And we should remember what an excellent navigator Captain Stuart has always been, too."

"Shortcake sure did a good job of tracking the place down for us," said Mason. "It's a real twist about the village, though." He looked over at Sarie. "You people been out there a long time."

"We had to start our own corporation, we're so far away- from the others. Lots of paperwork. Had to elect a president, too.

That's-the rules."

"Certainly sounds permanent," said the colonel. "And if I know Mason..."

"I wouldn't feel right kicking anybody off somewhere they grew up on." The carpenter rubbed another thoughtful hand over his whiskers. "Maybe we can make some kind of deal."

"I already did," said Gerald. "Didn't think you'd mind, old man, considering we'll all be in-laws, once Sarie and I get married. We want to live here at *The Last Resort*, anyway. Right?"

"What kind of deal?"

Gerald laughed (which made Sarie laugh), "That's the beauty of it!" He shook his head and smacked the table, again. "They keep on living the way they like, on their side, and we keep living the way we like over here on ours! If we do that— and this was the president's offer after talking it over with the elders—they'll keep us in supply of all the fish, crab, and meat we'll ever need. What I brought over today, is enough to last all winter."

"Sounds fair enough. Even seems a little

heavy on our end, considering the condition of the land. Maybe he just meant for a couple years, then we'd call it even. What with the price of meat these days."

"For as long as they're there and we're here. Talked it over, myself. Right Sarie?"

She smiled and nodded her head.

"I'd feel better if we could meet and shake hands on it." Mason rubbed at his whiskers, again.

At which point, Gerald's new fiancee stood up, leaned over the table, and held out her hand to him.

"Sarie's the president, Mase!" He smacked the table, again. "Nobody else wanted the job."

"Too much paperwork," said Sarie. "We like to share-meat, anyway. Specially, with in-laws."

"Oh, it all seems too good to be true!" Stella set the steaming kettle on a decorative ceramic tile in the center of the table, in case anyone wanted hot cider or tea. "Except for you not getting the restaurant you wanted to start there, Millie."

"I've got enough of a restaurant, right

here," she declared. "Look how many customers we've had, already, and the hunting season's still not over, yet. Besides, with Sammy and Mary making my Huckleberry Betty famous, that's all the advertising I need. Almost like having a franchise going in the next town, if you ask me. But how did Lou get anybody to believe her?"

"She looked up the property records over in Ketchikan to find out the exact location, then brought along a copy of the deed. Which, of course, has Mason's name on it. Then when she recognized your Huckleberry Betty recipe at the restaurant, Mil... that's when Sammy Robert told them they found all of us out here. She even left a letter for you before she went back, so you wouldn't worry."

"Lou wrote me a letter? Before Mase?"

"Yes, there's something in it she wanted you to be the first to know." Gerald reached into his pocket and retrieved a piece of paper that was simply folded over. "Of course, it's been read by the whole village, already. Without an envelope and all."

"I read-it twice," Sarie admitted, and giggled, again.

Millie sat down on the end of the bench and started to read, then burst into tears and handed it off to Mason to read out loud.

Dear Millie,

It's going to be a girl! I wanted to name her Princess Grace, for an extra advantage in life, but Cole said she had to have an ordinary name, too. So, we're going to call her Princess Grace Mildred DeForio, after the only mother I've ever known. Royal people have longer names, anyway.

Cap has a couple more weeks of therapy then we'll all be home for Christmas. Can you believe we've actually been on our own place all this time? How crazy is that? I really think it's a God thing!

Love,

Lou

PS: Don't worry, I've taken care of everybody's business and we still have money left over for Christmas presents. The colonel's going to get a big one!

Those few lines—as comforting as they were—didn't go a long way toward making any of them feel better about their finances. Typical of Lou Edna, it pleased and horrified at the same time. Especially the colonel, who—rather than anticipating the largest Christmas present, was worried the girl was going to spend all the money he had saved back so he and Stella could make a trip south in the spring, to try and salvage what was left of his writing career.

A thought so troublesome the two decided to stoke up the fire in their own quarters, even though it was late after the long, exciting visit (that included settling Sarie into one of the guest rooms) and talk over their options.

"I've come up with a Plan B," he informed her after she had changed into her pajamas and white terry robe with the Chinese collar (she loved getting comfortable before a cozy fire). He smacked his hands together and continued to pace in front of his desk. "Rather than airline tickets and hotels, we can pick up a second-hand RV and drive down. Even if we're at zero, we will have accrued enough by then to afford something. What do you think?"

"I think it's a wonderful idea, dear." She snuggled into her favorite spot on the couch, beneath the rose-colored afghan. "That would save us quite a bit on the accommodations for that conference you wanted to attend, too. The one you've been going to every year."

"That's right, I forgot about that. It would, indeed."

"And I should have a bit more saved up by then, too, don't forget. I'm actually glad I decided not to combine all my accounts before we left, till we changed states, instead. I only gave her one of my debit cards. Thank heavens!"

"Providential. I can see it, now."

"And she really does have a changed heart. Don't you think? So, maybe she'll feel a tap of conscience if she starts to get too extravagant. It is difficult to resist that Christmas shopping frenzy, though."

"God, help us!" It was an exasperated plea. "What on earth could she imagine I would need—at my age—that's big?"

"Maybe it was just a figure of speech," Stella offered. "Like if she buys us all bathrobes, yours would be biggest. Did she get you anything last year?"

"A bottle of Jim Beam I'm fairly certain she stole from some office party."

"Oh, but that was before she changed, so we can't count that."

"Still, the girl has no concept of money. That's something which takes time and experience. The right kind of experience, I mean. She's smart as a whip with numbers, and the inner workings of the banking industry. I can tell you that."

"At her age? Goodness, she's hardly twenty-three."

"She started young."

"Then I suppose we'll just have to wait and see."

9

Christmas at *The Last Resort* was a grand affair. At first it didn't seem as if the DeForio family would make it, considering it began to snow heavily again, on the day of Christmas Eve. However at the sound of an engine (this time, there was no mistaking the familiar thump of their diesel) early Christmas morning, as the *Mah-Bo II* chugged into the inlet, met by a pajama-and-jacket-clad group that formed the welcoming committee on the bridge. Stella got a lump in her throat at the squeal of delight from the Senator as he came riding up the path on Cole's shoulders and suddenly recognized where he was.

He reached out to Millie first, then burst into tears right along with her when she hugged him close (such a sensitive boy!). Then he had to hop from person-to-person and Stella got another lump in her throat just to feel those little arms around her neck, and that silky soft hair against her cheek when her turn came. His tiny black watch-cap (the same as his Uncle Gerald's), fell off in the tumult, and the rest of him was like hugging a pillow, since he was dressed in a blue snowsuit. Lou Edna brought up the rear, hanging onto the Captain, who insisted on walking himself (still aided by that familiar walking stick) rather than being hauled around like so much baggage over the shoulders of his First Mate.

It was a wonderful reunion.

No one went back to bed even though it was barely seven in the morning. Instead, they all retreated to the glass-enclosed stern deck (made from the extra panes scaled down from Gerald's greenhouse that had been moved ashore), decorated with twinkly lights and a tree, along with plenty of comfortable deck chairs for relaxing in. There was even a small wood stove —removed from the Chief Engineer's cabin—to keep the area warm and still be able to enjoy the winter views on three sides. There was a veritable mountain of presents under the tree, too.

The men had brought them in from the *Mah-Bo II*, while the women put on coffee and carried in all the specialties of the holiday breakfast they had prepared beforehand and only needed a quick warm-up. By the time everyone was settled and the Senator (in a new red bunny-suit, without holes in the knees) had happily claimed the unwrapped wooden train set under the tree... the time of reckoning had arrived.

"OK." Lou Edna started. "I know it's traditional for Pop to be Santa and hand out all the presents. But there's a lot of explaining that has to go with these, so I thought I better do the honors this year."

There was a heavy silence as everyone tried to imagine what their own money had bought themselves. Except for Sarie, who couldn't help giggling with a pleasure that transferred over to Gerald, too. Mostly out of nervousness. He never had much money but had confided earlier to Stella that he only hoped there would at least be enough left to buy Sarie a ring. The two of them were sitting together in a porch swing on the starboard end, that had been hung with chains from the ceiling, and had now become the most enjoyable spot out there.

"Mah-Bo," said Stuart (in a tone that clearly meant, get on with it) before taking a bite of biscuit that had smoked sausage and cheese baked into it.

"All right, I am," Lou Edna replied. "Cap wants me to do his first because it's the most important. Which, I'm sure you'll all agree. Let's see..." She turned to the tree. "I gotta find it, first."

At which point the Senator noticed the biscuit and sausage, and—almost without thinking—let go of the end of Mason's deck chair he had been holding onto with one hand, while playing with the train engine in the other, and began to totter across the short space to Stuart. They were his first steps. The women gasped and held their breath, and the two men sat forward, ready to catch, should he fall during the journey. There were no slip-ups. Other than flinging himself with total confidence onto the single arm held out to him that Stuart caught him up with to bring him safely onto his lap.

"Mah-Bo!" He laughed, and gave over the rest of his biscuit to the little hands. Then ruffled the child's dark curls and whispered, "Mah-Bo."

"Hey..." Cole got to his feet. "Hey, Cap..."

"His first steps!" Millie cried.

"What?" Lou Edna came out from behind the tree with a box in her hand. "I turn my back for two seconds and I missed it? Do it, again, for Mama, baby—I want to see this!"

But the moment had passed, as he was now more interested in the biscuit. However, the Captain and his First Mate had locked eyes over the top of the boy's head.

"I know what it means," the younger man told him. "I get it."

The Captain smiled a satisfied smile and leaned back in his chair as if greatly relieved. Lou Edna cleared her throat, and for a moment, Stella thought the girl was going to get emotional too. But she tucked a few loose strands of blonde hair behind one ear, took a deep breath, and recovered herself.

"I guess that's about as perfect an

introduction as there is. Hmm." She cleared her throat, again. "Anyway. This..." She handed the square box to her husband. "Is from Cap to Cole. And I want you all to know that it took me almost an hour last night for him to explain it to me. I mean, for me to understand what he was trying to explain. Open it up, Cole!"

"For me, huh..." Her husband winked at her from across the room. "I haven't had a Christmas present since I was a kid. Thanks, Cap. I hope it's not a—" He took the lid off the box and saw the Captain's old battered hat lying inside.

"It's a promotion!" Lou Edna exclaimed to his sudden silence. "You're the captain of the *My Boy II*! That's what it means, Cole. Mah-Bo means my boy!"

He didn't take it out of the box right away. Instead, he reached out slowly to shake hands with the old man, then bent down to give him a hug, instead. "I knew what it meant when I saw you pick up the boy, just now. I'll never let you down, sir. I swear."

"You're smarter than me," Lou Edna declared. "He had to spell it out with the alphabet blocks I was wrapping up for Buddy last night, before I got it right."

The boy flashed a glance back at his mother when she spoke the name he was finally beginning to recognize as his own.

"Ooops!" She covered her mouth for a moment, and then wagged a finger at the child. "But you don't know what those are, yet, do you. Have to wait and see."

So, the pile of unusual gifts began to diminish. Each one well chosen, turned out to be some thoughtful—not too expensive—token of Lou Edna's special appreciation for each family member. There was a new clip for Millie's lovely auburn hair, along with a home permanent kit the girl promised to take the hours to apply for her. For Mason, a set of lined work overalls (for the really cold days), and for Gerald, a packet of heirloom seeds that came from an apple tree next to George and Martha Washington's estate, ordered specially from a seed catalog. For Stella, there was a first edition autobiography of Mary Roberts Rinehart, that much-loved American version of Agatha Christie.

The larger boxes turned out to belong

mostly to the Senator (aka Buddy). Big bouncy balls, a riding scoot-along toy that looked like a tugboat, and various other things that would keep him entertained throughout the winter. With each reduction, they all breathed much easier, since no matter what she had bought for the colonel—barring a villa in the south of France— it couldn't possibly bankrupt everybody. Still, Stella could sense that her husband was practically beside himself, worrying over it. Especially since the small box remaining could not possibly hold a bathrobe. There was nothing big about it, at all.

"And now for our wonderful Mr. Colonel!" Lou Edna's eyes were especially bright and mischievous as she picked up the package. "First of all, I have to say how many times you made me nervous when I was sure you knew I was..." She thought for a moment. "Taking advantage of everybody. You won't believe how many times I was worried you were going to tell."

"Well, I thought about it," he admitted, "but there was always something that constrained me."

"I really didn't like you, back then."

"I understand completely."

"But—man—you were the most patient guy in the world. I tried so hard to irritate you, but you never fell for it."

"Oh, you irritated me many times, Lou." He admitted that, too.

Please, Lord, Stella prayed silently, let it be something inexpensive, like a wallet. Or, an item she stole from him and is trying to give back, maybe? The thought of anyone hurting her wonderful husband in any way was almost unbearable (he was such a good man!).

"But you forgave me for all that. I mean really forgave me." She thumped the slender box against her palm as she thought about it for a moment. "And then you trusted me. I don't know why. Pop and Millie—they love me. I don't know why, either, they just do. But you're the first person in my whole life who ever trusted me. So. I was trying to think of something special for you. Except you seem to have everything, already, and don't really need anything. Then I got this amazing idea. I actually think it was a God thing.

Anyway..." She handed him the box. "Merry Christmas."

"Thank you, my dear," he replied. "I'll treasure those words." He began to take off the wrapping. "And whatever this is, I'm sure it will be the perfect expression of who you are, in every way."

She smiled the sweetest smile of satisfaction (that girl really did have a good heart!) and finally went to sit down next to her little family while the colonel opened the box and looked inside. It was several folded sheets of paper. Stella leaned over his shoulder to see and as he unfolded them, a check fluttered onto his lap.

"What? What's this..." He grabbed Stella's hand and leapt to his feet, pulling her up with him. "It's—good heavens, girl—it's for twenty-five thousand dollars! Where did—"

"Read the papers!" Lou laughed out loud.

Soon everyone else had gotten up, too, and crowded around him.

"Dear Colonel Henry, Thank you for your decision to become one of our authors of fine literature for boys... But I only sent

them a query, halfway through Canada."

"Keep reading." prompted Lou.

"*It is a privilege to have someone of your distinction to work with, who is willing to take on this special calling to help raise the standards of today's young people.* I don't recall any such —"

"Go on, go on," Now it was Gerald who interrupted. "I say, the suspense is excruciating. A bona fide advance—it's simply splendid!"

"*Enclosed, you will find the advance against royalties we agreed upon...* But I never did!"

"I'll explain later," the girl insisted.

"*...with the final installment to be paid on submission of the completed first manuscript,* First manuscript? *...previously discussed,* Now, I know I never discussed anything... *and spelled out in your copy of the contract.*" He flipped to the next page (it was certainly a contract), then back, again, to hurry through the final words. "*Welcome to you and these wonderful characters you have created. We will look forward to many years of adventures, together.* Many years—good

Lord—did you hear that, Stella?"

"I certainly did—many years!"

"*Sincerely, E.F. Coffman, Editor in Chief...*" He turned to the last page and looked at the signature that he definitely recognized as his own. "I'm thunderstruck! In a wonderful sort of way but this is entirely impossible. I never in my life signed such a thing!"

"I signed it for you."

"Lou—Edna—DeForio!" Millie gasped and reached into the pocket of her robe for her heart pills. "You. Of all people, should know what forgery is!"

"It's a felony. But Millie, only if someone presses charges. And I knew—under the circumstances— he would want me to! Now, everybody just listen. First thing I did after we got to Ketchikan, was get a P.O. Box and get our mail started up, again. That was on the list, remember? After a couple weeks a big batch of it came through."

"It's against the law to read other people's mail, too," Mason pointed out. "Under any circumstances."

"But there was important stuff in there,

Pop. A lot of it had to be dealt with right away, and Cap needed four more weeks of therapy. Four weeks! With no way to get hold of any of you. Besides that, we were getting ready to go looking for the lodge and who knew how long that would take? We didn't even know when we'd get back to Ketchikan, again, much less all the way back here. Millie, if I hadn't ordered you more heart pills, right then? They never would have got there before we left."

"I have been running low on those. I was thinking about that, last week."

"There was lots of stuff like that. But this thing with the colonel—it was time sensitive. I mean, who knows how much paperwork had to go back and forth, or if he took too long to answer and they filled up those slots with somebody else's books?"

"Most definitely could have occurred if I never showed up, again," conceded the colonel.

"See? You did need somebody to handle things for you. That's what agents do. Right? I was sort of like one of those. So, I went ahead and made the deal. A pretty good one, too. If you ask me."

"It's an excellent deal," he agreed. "As long as I don't have to write six books in a year."

"Six books in two."

"It's tight, but I can manage it." He put an arm around Stella and hugged her close. "Now that I have Stel."

"Whew! That's the only part I was a little worried about."

"Well..." Then he laughed at the sheer relief and pleasure of it all. "Lou Edna, I can't thank you enough!"

"Enough to give me fifteen percent? That's what agents get, I looked it up."

"I'll give you ten."

"Woo—hoo!" She looked over her shoulder, where her husband was standing behind her. "See, Cole? I told you he would!"

He wrapped his arms around her, more as if holding her still than giving her a hug. "All I could see was having to come up with bail money." Then he leaned his forehead against the back of her hair with sigh of relief. "Girl, you gotta—quit this kinda stuff!"

"But, now we can start saving for our

fishing license." It was a piece of news that had obviously slipped out, and she quickly scanned the circle of questioning faces around them. "It takes a whole lot of money to fish in this state," she explained.

Cole tightened his hold on her.

"Which we are going to earn every penny of. Ourselves," she assured. At which point she caught Mason's doubtful eye and insisted, "I really mean it, Pop."

"Meanwhile, what happens when the colonel has to sign his real signature on something?" Millie suddenly wanted to know.

"Not a problem, Mil. I've been signing everybody's signatures for years."

Millie automatically reached for the toddler who was pulling at her bathrobe, and lifted him onto her hip before giving an exasperated sigh. "Lou Edna, it'll be a miracle—an out and out miracle—if I even live to seventy, trying to figure you out!"

"You got-the best family I ever saw, Gerry," Sarie observed out loud.

"They're always like this," he replied. "You're going to love it here!"

Exactly the way I have, Stella thought to herself as she looked around the happy room. It was the first Christmas she had spent with a real family in many years. Then it occurred to her how her new life had started during the holiday season, exactly one year ago. Goodness, the Lord had brought her a long way on one simple prayer! She looked up at the colonel, who had risked everything he owned (to rescue her way back then) and wondered if he had any idea...

It had been his finest hour.

Author's Note

Winston Churchill (who was quoted at the beginning of this story) had to overcome many obstacles in his life. More than the average person. Born into a wealthy family with a long line of ancestors who had significantly contributed to England's history, he felt—from an early age—the burden to do something significant, too. However, he was often in trouble at school, did not excel in most of his classes, and also had a speech impediment. He was overly emotional, as well, and fought bouts of depression throughout his entire life.

When his father died at the age of forty-five, and seeing that many of the men in his family had a tendency to die young, he assumed the same thing would happen to himself. Which led him to believe that if he was going to make any mark in life, it would have to be while he was young. And the only place to do that was in the military. So, he joined the rifle corps at the age of fourteen, went to military school (he had to try three times before passing the entrance exam), and for the next twenty-nine years, volunteered for every battlefield he heard about.

During this time, he also became a war correspondent for several newspapers and—having been deployed to Cuba, India, the Middle East, Africa, and the Western Front (during World War I)—also wrote books about those campaigns. By the age of twenty-six he had seen action fifty times, been captured as a prisoner of war and escaped, and become popular all over the country both for his bravery, as well as for his accurate descriptions and insights of these battlefields. It was also at this age that he campaigned for—and won—his first seat in Parliament.

Throughout the following years, Churchill was involved both in politics and wars, during which he made some significant gains and many equally significant mistakes. When he finally retired, he was at the lowest ebb of his life. A period which was later to become known as his "wilderness years."

He retreated to his country home to quietly continue his writing. He had done some good. And he had lived nearly twenty years longer than his father. He was done. Finished. However, when the country slipped into crisis, then the Great Depression—and finally—stood on the very brink of another World War, he was offered the post of Prime Minister. England's highest and most powerful office. Something of an accomplishment in itself, except the country was already in a state that was almost too desperate to survive. So, suddenly— when he least expected it—Winston Churchill was faced with his own "finest hour."

And he was up to it.

Today, he is remembered for his steadfast refusal to consider defeat, surrender, or a compromised peace. Ideals which helped inspire British resistance during the difficult early days of the war when Britain stood alone against Hitler. He is particularly noted for his speeches and radio broadcasts which continued to inspire them until victory over Nazi Germany was secured.

Named the Greatest Briton of all time in a 2002 poll, Churchill is still widely regarded as being among the most influential people in British history. One of the best paid writers of his time, he was also awarded the Nobel Prize for Literature, "for his mastery of historical and biographical description as well as for brilliant oratory in defending exalted human values."

He lived to the age of ninety. You can read more about this inspiring man, for free at many places online.

About Lilly Maytree...

Lilly Maytree is the author of Gold Trap, The Pandora Box, and The Stella Madison Capers. Books that sent her careening along on her "Mystery Tours" with her captain husband aboard the Glory B. She loves sharing these adventures with readers. It has even been said that she time-travels (but that's probably just a rumor). To find out about her current adventures, simply visit:

LillyMaytree.com

You can get in touch with her by sending an email to: lilly@LillyMaytree.com. It might take a few days if she is adventuring far away... but she always comes back sooner or later.

Other Books by
Lilly Maytree

Novels...

Gold Trap

Megan Jennings is headed to Africa for high adventure and divine appointments until she makes a small wrong turn. But what is faith, if not to strike out against impossible odds believing you will win? Or leap out into the dark knowing someone will be there to catch you? Someone does catch her... but it isn't who she was expecting.

The Pandora Box

Journalist D.J. Parker learns the location of a famous cache of diamonds that were stolen during World War II. What she doesn't know is— the federal government has been following the case for years. With an old journal to lead the way, she sets out aboard a yacht that once carried the infamous Herman Goering. A thrilling treasure hunt that could either prove to be the adventure of a lifetime... or her worst nightmare.

Home Before Dark
(Caper #1)

Here is the first of the Stella Madison Capers, the story of how everything started, and how she escaped from a catastrophe that seemed to come out of nowhere. Which is the nature of catastrophes but it's so hard to be logical when you're in the middle of one. It's also the story of how she met the colonel (if you're interested in that sort of thing).

A Thief in the House
(Caper #2)

Stella Madison is back, this time with a bevy of friends. But just how far should a person go when it comes to sticking by their friends? There's a thief in the rambling old mansion she moved into. And while it was someone who was quick to lend help when Stella needed it most, how can she possibly return the favor without jeopardizing herself along with them? No person is obligated to go that far... right?

Voyage of the Dreadnaught
Collection of four Stella Madison Capers

Here is a collection of the four Stella Madison Capers covering the entire voyage of the *Dreadnaught*, through the Inside Passage to Alaska. Includes: **Sea Trials**, **The Pushover Plot**, **Lost in the Wilderness**, and **The Last Resort**. Also includes a brief account of Lilly Maytree's true-life voyage along the same route, in the sailboat *Glory B.*

The Complete Stella Madison Capers

A collection of all six Stella Madison Capers in one place, for those who enjoy reading the whole story all the way through, or would simply rather keep things more neatly together.

For Writers...

Unspoken Rules

Popular books (those stories everyone likes no matter what the subject) all have certain things in common. And what they have most in common is what they DON'T do. Within the following pages, dear writer, you will find the three most important "don'ts" of popular fiction that I learned when I was studying the masters. Why? Because I love research and I never mind sharing my notes.

Writing Rules!
(a mysterious student handbook)

A mysterious little desktop handbook that can help anyone (well, almost anyone) with writing rules. Especially if you are a student and have to write things all the time.

For Parents...

Behave Yourself!
Teaching your children to discipline themselves.

Are you tired of bickering during daily routines encroaching on way too much of your family time? Here is a book that offers a two- week program that teaches your children to discipline themselves. Hard to believe? Here are the step-by-step secrets of how it's done, and why it works.

The Nature of Children
(And how to deal with it.)

A manual based on a compilation of parenting articles Lilly wrote over several years as a columnist for Childcare Magazine. It is a result of many requests from parents for more information about that content and the foundation of the methods she used both in raising her own children, and in her classrooms.

After years of experience, she has a lot to say about what motivates children and has implemented many of her unique ideas into books and programs that others can use.

For autographed copies, visit:

www.LillyMaytree.com

To read more books like this,
visit us online at:

LightsmithPublishers.com

Also available from Ingram
wherever books are sold.

If you enjoyed reading this
"Little Traveling Book"
please share it with someone!

If you have children (or know any),
you may even enjoy browsing the
"mysteriously different books" over at:

SummersIslandPress.com